The Emperor's New Clothes

D1636062

Illustrated by Sherry Neidigh

Adapted by Mary Rowitz

Louis Weber, C.E.O.
Publications International, Ltd.
7373 North Cicero Avenue
Lincolnwood, Illinois 60646

Manufactured in U.S.A.

ISBN: 0-7853-1922-0

PUBLICATIONS INTERNATIONAL, LTD.
Stories to Grow On is a trademark of Publications International, Ltd.

There once lived an emperor who loved clothes more than anything else. His clothes filled closets and even entire rooms in the royal palace.

The emperor selected only the finest fabrics and hired the finest tailors to work for him. He was very rich, and that was a good thing because he spent a lot of money on clothes.

The emperor also spent a lot of money on mirrors. He thought that his fancy clothes made him look quite dashing, so he spent most of his time preening in front of the palace mirrors.

The emperor's pride was well-known throughout the kingdom. The people thought him quite silly to spend so much time in front of his mirrors, but they never said so to his face. He was, after all, their emperor.

Word of the emperor reached two thieves in a faraway land. Instead of making jokes about him, they decided to use the emperor's pride to make themselves rich.

The thieves dressed up as traveling tailors and made the long journey to the emperor's palace. They told the palace guards they had the most wonderful fabric in all the world, and asked for permission to show it to the emperor.

The sneaky tailors explained to the emperor and his wife that their fabric was not only wonderful, but magical, too. "Only the wisest people in the land will see this fabric, Your Majesty," they said. "It will be invisible to fools or those who are unfit for their office."

When the tailors opened their bags, the emperor squinted. He saw nothing at all in their hands! "Why, I must be a fool," the emperor thought. "Either that or I do not deserve to sit on this throne!"

The emperor asked his wife what she thought of the fabric. "It is the most beautiful fabric I have ever seen," she said uneasily.

Knowing his wife was no fool, the emperor offered the tailors twenty pieces of gold to make him a new suit. The tailors thanked the emperor and went right to work.

"When you wear this suit, Your Majesty, it will feel as light as a spider's web against your skin," one tailor said as he measured to the top of the emperor's head. "You might even feel as though you're wearing nothing at all."

"Indeed, this must be the most wonderful fabric in the world!" the emperor said.

The tailors smiled slyly and winked at each other behind the emperor's back. They had finished sizing him up.

After a few days, the royal minister went to check on the tailors' progress. The minister was stunned by what he didn't see. The tailors were cutting away at the air with their scissors and stitching up fabric that wasn't there! "Is it possible that I am a fool?" the minister gulped.

Seeing the minister, one of the tailors said, "Please tell the emperor his suit will be ready soon. But first, please order us another tray of food. All this hard work is making us very hungry."

That much must be true, the minister thought as he saw apple cores, chicken legs, and bits of cheese all over the floor. The tailors must be working hard on something!

Finally the tailors brought the emperor his new suit. He put it on slowly, careful not to snag the fine stitching he couldn't see. Then he strutted around the room. He had never felt so dashing.

"This is truly the finest suit I have ever had," the emperor said to the royal minister.

"If you are happy, then I am happy," said the royal minister, who was truly anything but happy. In his eyes, the emperor was standing in front of a mirror in his underwear, admiring a new suit that wasn't even there!

The emperor wanted to show off his new suit to all the people in the land. He asked the royal minister to call for a royal parade the next day.

The people were excited about the parade, too. They had long ago grown bored with stories of the emperor's clothes, but what interested them now was the new magical fabric. Everyone wanted to find out which among them were fools.

On the day of the parade, everyone pushed and shoved to get the best view. But when the emperor appeared, the people were shocked. The emperor was in his underwear! No one in the crowd could see the emperor's suit, but no one would say so out loud. No one wanted to look like a fool. Instead the people said, "How handsome you look, Your Majesty!"

Suddenly a young boy cried out over the crowd. "The emperor isn't wearing a new suit!" he said. "What is everybody talking about? All the emperor is wearing is his underwear!"

The emperor quickly turned to the people. They stood in stunned silence. Instantly, the emperor knew the boy was telling the truth. He realized that he had been a fool, and now he was sitting before his people in his underwear.

The people in the crowd began to laugh. They realized that they had been foolish, too. The people had pretended to see a suit which did not exist. They were afraid of what the others would think if they told the emperor the truth.

When the emperor returned to the palace, he ignored all his fancy and frilly clothes and put on a simple blue robe with plain yellow buttons. "That's better," he said, slipping on the robe. For the first time, the emperor left his room without looking in the mirror. Then he invited the honest young boy to his court.

"I have decided to make you a junior minister. You risked being called a fool to tell me the truth," the emperor said. "You will always be one of my most trusted friends."

"Thank you, Your Majesty," the boy said. "I will always be honest with you, even if you don't like what I have to say."

One to Grow On

Honesty

Even a great emperor can learn a lot about honesty from a little boy. Sometimes being honest means telling people things they don't want to hear. Have you ever been afraid to tell someone the truth? It's not always easy, and sometimes it's even scary. But no matter how difficult it is, telling the truth is important. If the little boy had not told the emperor the truth, the emperor might still be ruling the kingdom in his underwear!